THE ULTIMATE

Snake

BOOK FOR KIDS

Find us on **YouTube** for weekly animal videos just for kids!

Join us on YouTube

BELLANOVA

MELBOURNE · SOFIA · BERLIN

ISBN: 978-2-487191-20-4
Imprint: Bellanova Books

Contents

Introduction

Are you ready to dive into the amazing and slithery world of snakes?

From the tiny **thread snake** to the giant **anaconda**, snakes are some of the most fascinating creatures on our planet.

They come in all shapes, sizes, and colors, and they live in almost every corner of the world. Whether you're curious about how snakes hunt, where they live, or why they shed their skin, you're in for an adventure!

In this book, we'll answer all your questions about these cool reptiles, including:

- How can snakes smell
  with their tongues?

- How snake can a swallow prey
  bigger than its head?!

- Why are some snakes
  super venomous while others
  are as harmless as a kitten?

We'll explore snake habitats from hot deserts to dense rainforests, and we'll meet some famous snakes you might already know, like the king cobra and the python. Plus, we'll uncover some surprising and lesser-known species that will blow your mind!

But that's not all! We've packed this book with awesome pictures, fun activities, and quizzes to test your snake smarts. You'll even learn how to be safe around snakes and why they're so important to our world.

So grab your magnifying glass and
your explorer hat, and let's embark
on a thrilling journey into the world of
ssspectacular snakes.

What is a snake?

Let's kick off our journey by figuring out what makes a snake a snake. Snakes are a type of reptile, which means they're cold-blooded and covered in scales, just like lizards and crocodiles. But there's something pretty special about snakes: they don't have legs! Instead, they slither and slide on their bellies using their muscles and scales. Pretty cool, right?

FUN FAST FACTS ABOUT SNAKES:

No Legs, No Problem: Even without legs, snakes can move quickly and gracefully. Some can climb trees or even swim!

Big Mouths: Snakes have incredibly flexible jaws that allow them to open their mouths wide and swallow prey larger than their heads.

Scaly Skin: Those shiny scales covering a snake's body help protect it and keep it smooth for easy movement.

Unique Senses: Snakes don't hear like we do, but they can sense vibrations through the ground and have a special way of smelling by flicking their tongues in and out.

Snake Anatomy

Discover what's inside and outside a snake's body!

Did you know?

Some snakes can dislocate their jaws to eat prey larger than their head!

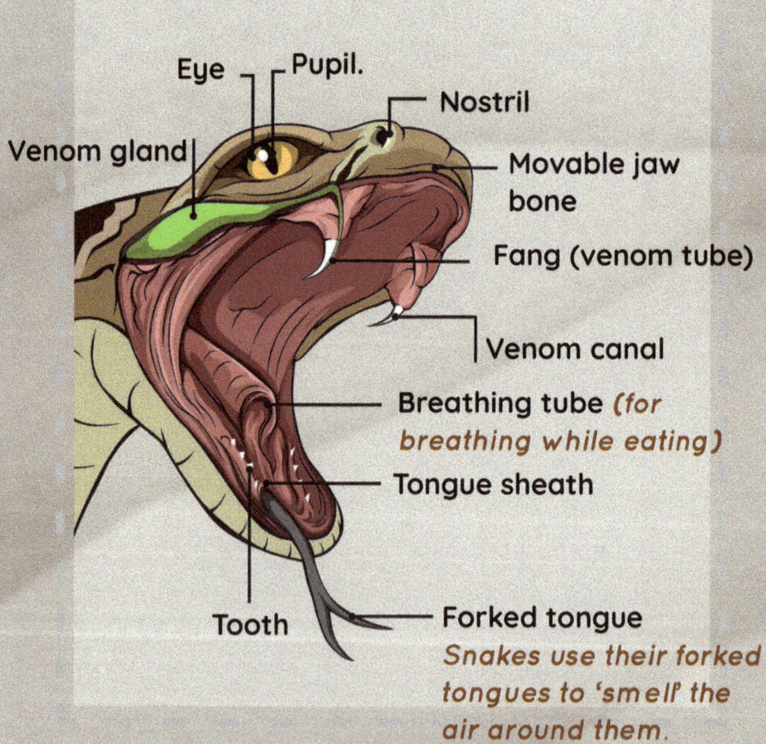

Forked tongue
Snakes use their forked tongues to 'smell' the air around them.

Did you know?

Snake tails serve many purposes! Rattlesnakes use their rattle to warn predators. Tree-dwelling snakes, like boas, use their tails to grip branches. Some snakes can even lose part of their tail to escape predators, and it can regrow!

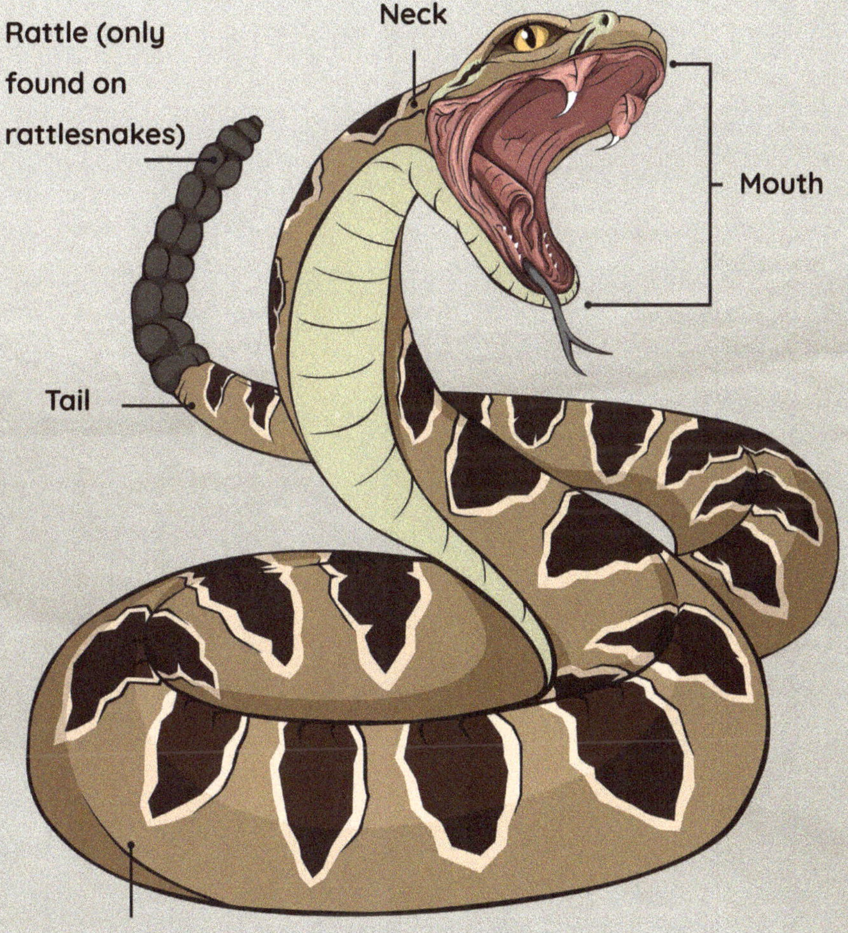

Body scales. *A snake's scales can be smooth or rough, helping them blend into their environment.*

Snake senses
How snakes see, smell, hear & feel

Discover how snakes navigate their world using their unique senses! From incredible vision to their ability to "taste" the air, snakes have some truly amazing ways of understanding their environment.

Vision

Snake eyes are covered by a clear scale called a **brille**, which protects them. Snakes don't have great vision. Their sight is adapted more for detecting movement than for detailed viewing.

Nocturnal snakes, which hunt at night, and crepuscular snakes, which are active at dawn or dusk, usually have **vertical pupils**.

Diurnal snakes, active during the day, typically have **round pupils**.

Smell

Snakes can 'smell' with their tongues! They use their forked tongues to collect scent particles from the air and ground. They bring these particles to a special organ in their mouth called the **Jacobson's organ**, which helps them "smell" their surroundings.

The forked tongue also gives snakes a kind of stereo smell, helping them determine the direction of a scent.

Touch

Since a snake's body is so elongated, it's almost always in contact with the ground.

The scales on a snake's belly are very sensitive and contain receptors that help them feel the texture and temperature of the ground.

They can feel the tiniest vibrations in the ground, helping them avoid danger and find prey.

Black western whip snake.

Hearing

Snakes don't have outer ears but have a middle ear bone that connects to their jaw, allowing them to sense vibrations. Different species react differently to sounds: some, like the **Woma Python**, move towards sounds, while others, like the **Taipan**, move away.

Their powerful internal ears pick up low-frequency vibrations. While humans hear a wide range of sounds between 20 and 20,000 Hz, snakes can detect vibrations between 50 and 1,000 Hz.

The Boiga snake, also known as the cat snake, is native to Asia, India and Australia.

Snake Habitats

Snakes live on every continent except Antarctica, so they've had to learn to adapt to some very extreme environments.

Fortunately, snakes are incredibly adaptable creatures. From dense forests to arid deserts, and even in oceans, snakes have evolved to thrive in a variety of environments. In this chapter, we'll explore the different habitats where snakes live and learn about the amazing adaptations that help them survive.

FOREST SNAKES

Forests are vibrant ecosystems full of life and provide a diverse range of habitats for snakes. These environments offer plenty of cover and abundant prey, making them ideal for many snake species.

Forests can be tropical, temperate, or boreal, each hosting different kinds of snakes adapted to the specific conditions.

Scientific name: Morelia viridis

Habitat: Rainforests in New Guinea, Indonesia & Australia.

Adaptations: Uses its bright green color to hide among the leaves, waiting to ambush prey.

Some forest snakes can glide from tree to tree! The paradise tree snake flattens its body to catch the air and glide to another tree.

Adaptations

CAMOUFLAGE

Many forest snakes have green or brown scales that blend perfectly with the leaves and branches. This helps them stay hidden from both predators and prey.

TREE-CLIMBING SKILLS

Tree-dwelling snakes have strong tails and muscles that allow them to climb and move easily among the trees.

Desert Snakes

Despite extreme temperatures and little water, special snake species such as the **Sidewinder** have adapted to make the scorching desert their home.

SURVIVAL SECRETS

- **Nocturnal:** Many desert snakes hunt at night when it's cooler. This helps them avoid the extreme heat of the day.

- **Water Conservation:** Desert snakes have efficient kidneys to hold water, allowing them to survive in an environment with very little water.

- **Burrowing:** Some desert snakes burrow into the sand to escape the heat and predators. The **Sidewinder snake** has it's own adaptation too: it moves sideways across the hot desert sand to stay cool and avoid sinking!

Some desert snakes brumate (see pg. 52) during the cold desert winters.

Credit: AH, Krisp

Horned desert viper

Scientific name: Cerastes cerastes

Habitat: Deserts of Northern Africa, such as the Sahara Desert.

Adaptation Highlight: Uses its horns for camouflage and ambush hunting. Their sandy-colored bodies also help them blend into the sand.

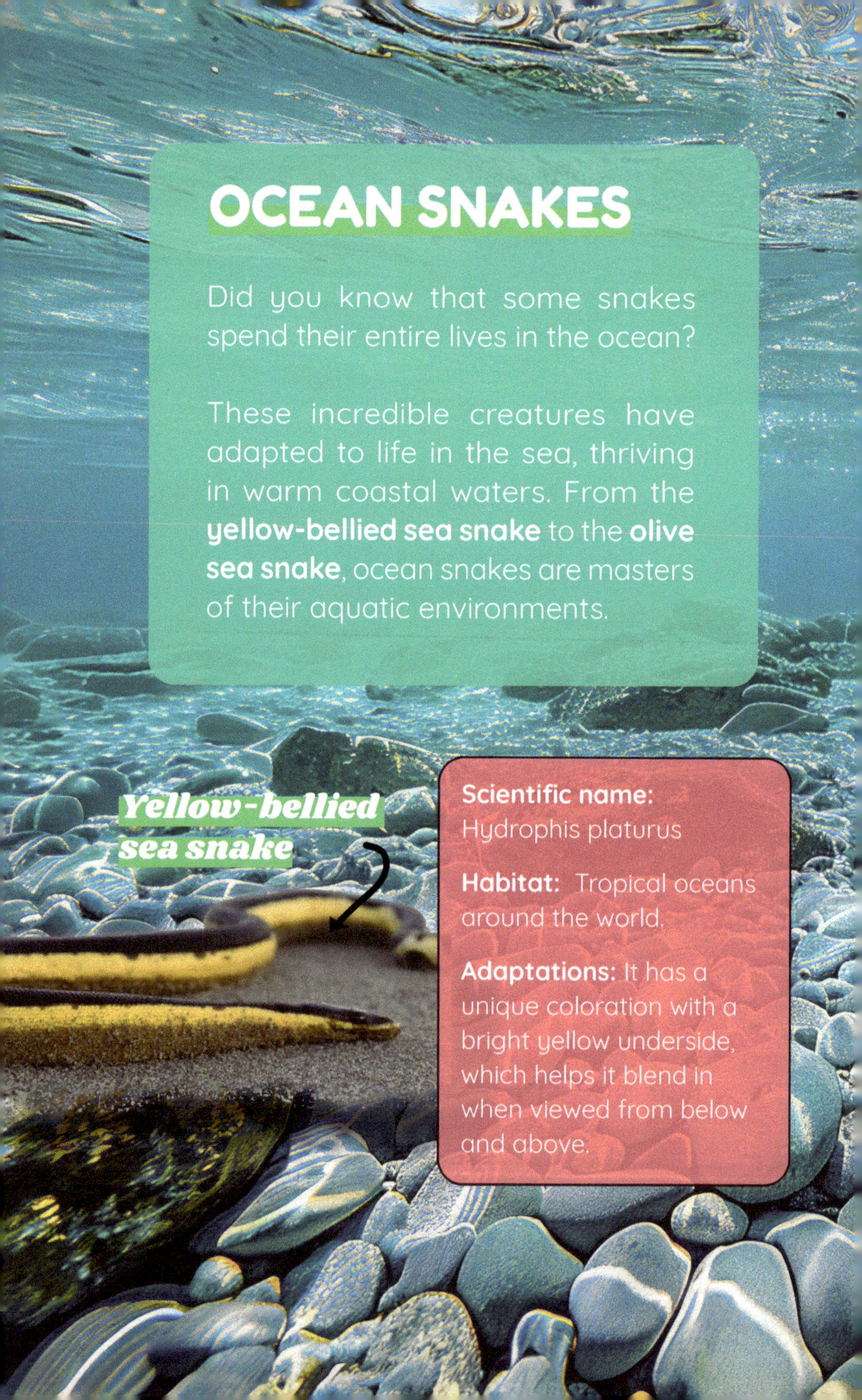

OCEAN SNAKES

Did you know that some snakes spend their entire lives in the ocean?

These incredible creatures have adapted to life in the sea, thriving in warm coastal waters. From the **yellow-bellied sea snake** to the **olive sea snake**, ocean snakes are masters of their aquatic environments.

Scientific name: Hydrophis platurus

Habitat: Tropical oceans around the world.

Adaptations: It has a unique coloration with a bright yellow underside, which helps it blend in when viewed from below and above.

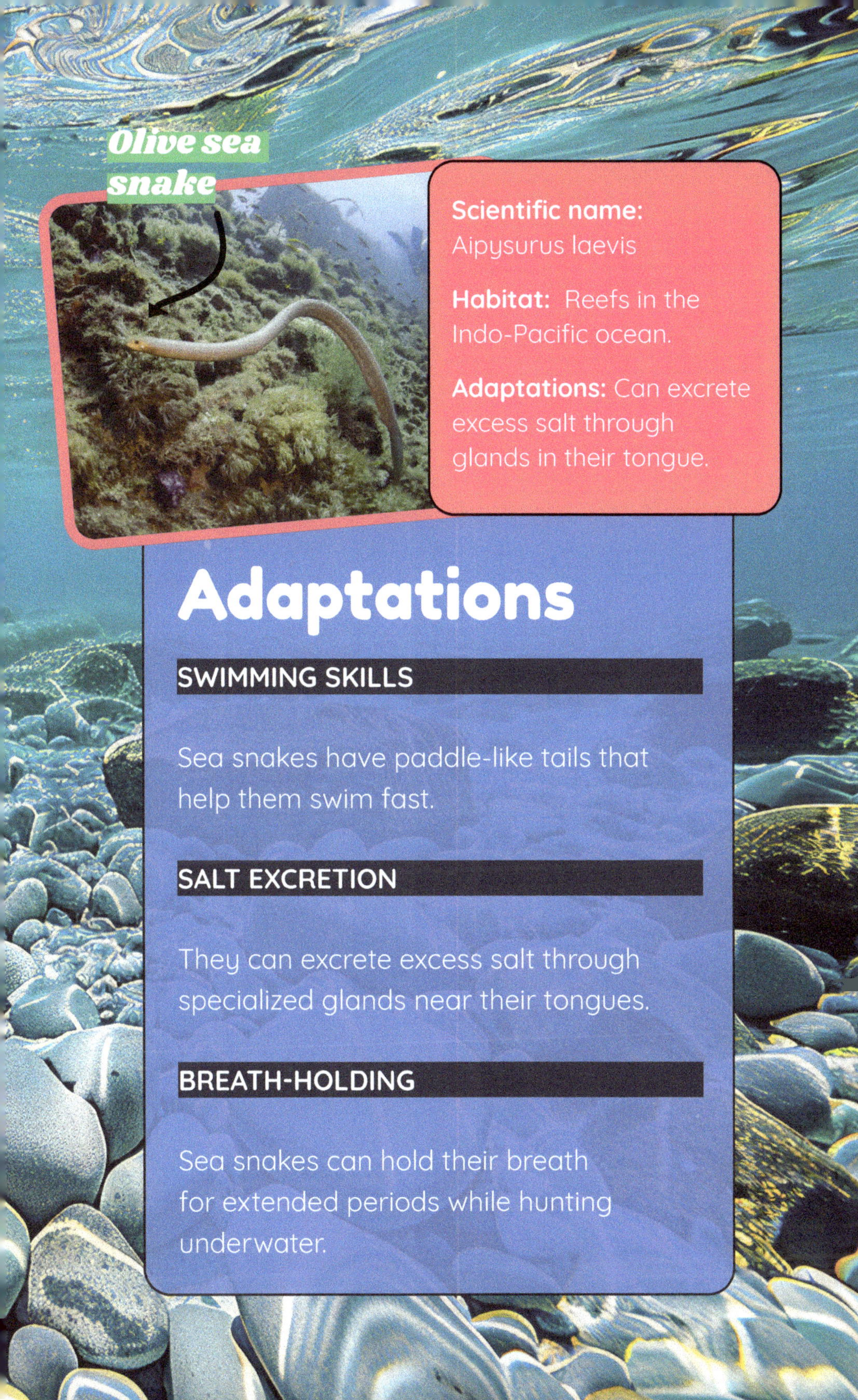

Scientific name: Aipysurus laevis

Habitat: Reefs in the Indo-Pacific ocean.

Adaptations: Can excrete excess salt through glands in their tongue.

Adaptations

SWIMMING SKILLS

Sea snakes have paddle-like tails that help them swim fast.

SALT EXCRETION

They can excrete excess salt through specialized glands near their tongues.

BREATH-HOLDING

Sea snakes can hold their breath for extended periods while hunting underwater.

Venomous vs Non-venomous

Snakes come in all shapes and sizes, and not all of them are venomous. Only about 15% of all snake species are venomous, and only 7% have venom strong enough to harm humans.

Identifying venomous snakes isn't always easy. Always keep a safe distance and tell an adult if you see a snake. Never approach it.

Pupil Shape

It's a myth that pupil shape can tell you whether a snake is venomous or non-venomous. Instead, they usually indicate whether a snake is **diurnal** or **nocturnal**.

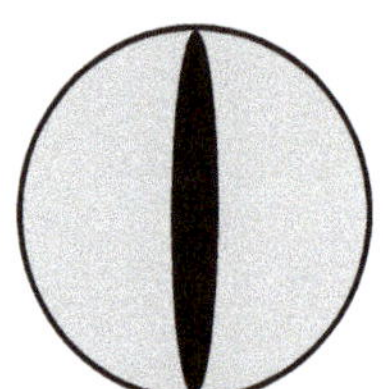

Slit-like pupils

Round pupils

< A non-venomous Gonyosoma snake.

Head shape

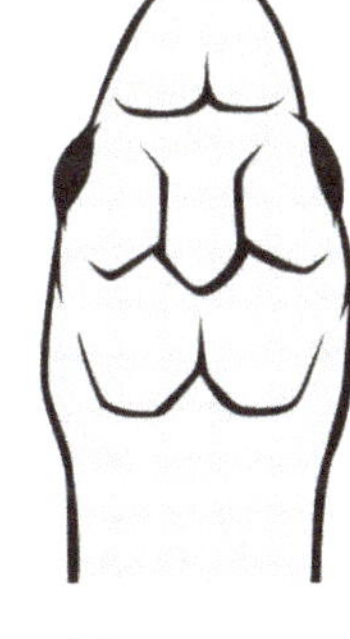

Non-venomous **Venomous**

Venomous snakes often have a more triangular head shape due to their venom glands, while non-venomous snakes tend to have a more rounded head.

Body shape & color

Venomous snakes often have thicker, more muscular bodies compared to their non-venomous counterparts.

Some venomous snakes have bright, contrasting color patterns as a warning. However, this is not a foolproof method as many non-venomous snakes mimic these patterns.

< The Copperheaded trinket snake is venomous.

Snake Species

With over 3,000 different species of snake spread around the globe, these remarkable reptiles display an incredible variety of shapes, sizes, colors, and behaviors.

From the massive **green anaconda** of the Amazon to the elusive **eastern coral snake** of North America, each species has its own story to tell.

While we can't look at them all, we've picked out some of the coolest ones we know.

A blue viper.

KING COBRA

Scientific name:
Ophiophagus hannah

Habitat: Forests in India and Southeast Asia

Length: Up to 18 ft (5.5 m)

Danger Score: 4/5
The king cobra has very strong venom and can deliver a lot of it in one bite.

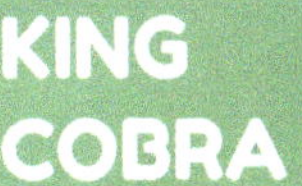

YELLOW ANACONDA

Scientific name:
Eunectes notaeus

Habitat: Swamps and marshes in South America

Length: Up to 13 ft (4 m)

Danger Score: 2/5
The yellow anaconda can constrict its prey very tightly, but it's not usually aggressive towards humans.

© Patrick Jean

BLACK MAMBA

Scientific name: Dendroaspis polylepis

Habitat: Savannas in sub-Saharan Africa

Length: Up to 14 ft (4.3 m)

Danger Score: 5/5

The black mamba has extremely potent venom that can kill a human in just a few hours.

Did you know?!

Corn snakes are often mistaken for the venomous Copperhead due to their similar coloration.

CORN SNAKE

Scientific name: Pantherophis guttatus

Habitat: Forests, overgrown fields, and farmlands in the southeastern United States

Length: 2-6 ft (0.6-1.8 m)

Danger Score: 1/5

BLUE VIPER

Length: Up to 3 feet (0.9 meters)

Scientific name:
Trimeresurus insularis

Danger Score: 4/5
The Blue Viper has strong venom that can cause severe damage to its prey and can be very dangerous to humans.

Habitat: Forested areas, primarily on Komodo Island, Indonesia.

© Nick Evans

Eastern Brown Snake

Scientific name: Pseudonaja textilis

Habitat: Grasslands, woodlands, and urban areas in Australia

Length: Up to 6.6 ft (2 m)

Danger Score: 5/5

The eastern brown snake has extremely potent venom that can cause rapid paralysis and death if not treated quickly.

VENOMOUS

© Gihan Jayaweera

GREEN TREE PYTHON

Scientific name:
Morelia viridis

Habitat: Tropical rainforests of New Guinea, Indonesia, and Australia

Length: Up to 7 ft (2.1 m)

Danger Score: 1/5

© Sin Syue Li

RATTLESNAKE

Scientific name: Crotalus spp.

Habitat: Deserts, grasslands, and forests in North and South America

Length: Up to 8 ft (2.4 m)

Danger Score: 3/5

Rattlesnakes have potent venom that can cause severe pain and tissue damage.

© Genjitsu

FORMOSAN ODD-SCALED SNAKE

Scientific name: Achalinus formosanus

Habitat: Taiwan and some islands in Japan

Length: Up to 14 ft (4.3 m)

Danger Score: 1/5

The Formosan Odd-Scaled Snake has iridescent scales that overlap irregularly, giving it a unique, shiny appearance.

SRI LANKAN FLYING SNAKE

Scientific name: Chrysopelea taprobanica

Length: Up to 3 ft (0.9 m)

Danger Score: 1/5

Habitat: Forests in Sri Lanka and parts of India

GABOON VIPER

Scientific name: Bitis gabonica

Habitat: Rainforests and savannas in sub-Saharan Africa

Length: Up to 7 ft (2.1 m)

Danger Score: 4/5

Its bite can cause severe pain, swelling, and tissue damage.

The Gaboon Viper has the longest fangs of any snake, reaching up to 2 in (5 cm) in length.

© Kevin Enge

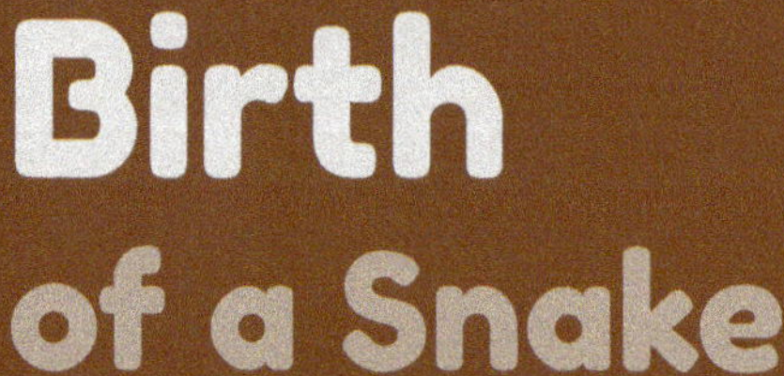

Birth
of a Snake

Let's take a look at how snakes start their lives.

Eggs or Live Birth?

The way a snake is born depends on its species. Some snakes, like the king cobra, lay eggs, while others, like the boa constrictor, give birth to live young.

Florida pine snakes hatching >

Baby snakes are born with all the instincts they need to survive on their own!

Once they are born, snakelets are ready to take on the world. They start exploring their surroundings and searching for their first meal.

All baby snakes are called **snakelets**. But if they are born from an egg they are called **hatchlings,** and the term **neonates** is used for live birth snakelets.

Did you know?

Some snake species can grow over a foot in their first year! A young snake's diet helps determine how fast and big it will grow.

A rat snake hatching.

Molting

As snakes grow, they need to shed their old skin to make room for new growth. This process is called molting, and it happens many times throughout a snake's life. When they're young, they may molt up to 12 times a year!

© Cotinis

How Do Snakes Molt?

Molting helps snakes grow and get rid of parasites. When their skin becomes dull, they rub themselves against a rough surface to remove the skin.

Did you know? Some snakes eat their shed skin to recycle nutrients!

Hunting & Diet

Snakes are fascinating predators with unique hunting skills and diverse diets. Let's dive into the world of snake hunting and discover what they eat and how they catch their prey.

Did you know?

Some snakes can strike their prey in less than a second!

Snakes use a variety of techniques to hunt and capture their prey. Some rely on stealth and camouflage, while others use speed and agility.

This smooth snake (*Coronella austriaca*) is in attack position.

Camouflage

Many snakes rely on their ability to blend into their surroundings to ambush unsuspecting prey.

Speed

Speed is crucial for snakes. They have to act fast to catch their prey and escape from predators. They use several types of movements including sidewinding, and pushing off from a surface using their muscles in a wave-like motion (*lateral undulation*).

The **black mamba** is one of the fastest snakes in the world, capable of moving at speeds up to 12 mph (20 km/h).

The Sidewinder rattlesnake can reach speeds of up to 18 mph (29 km/h), making it the fastest snake in the world!

The king cobra is not only the world's longest venomous snake, but it can move fast to escape danger, reaching speeds of up to 12 mph (20 km per hour).

Venom

Many snakes use venom to subdue their prey. Let's learn how venom works and why it's so effective.

HOW VENOM WORKS

Venom contains proteins that can immobilize or kill prey. Different snakes have different types of venom each adapted to their diet.

TYPES OF VENOM

There are two main types of venom: hemotoxic and neurotoxic. Each type affects the body differently.

Hemotoxic Venom:

- Affects the blood and tissues.
- Can cause swelling, pain, and tissue damage.
- **Examples:** Rattlesnakes and copperheads.

Neurotoxic Venom:

- Affects the nervous system.
- Can cause paralysis and breathing difficulties.
- **Examples:** Cobras and coral snakes.

Did you know?

A black mamba's venom is powerful enough to kill an elephant!

Diet

Snakes have a varied diet, depending on their species, size, and habitat. But all snakes are carnivores, meaning they only eat meat.

Small Mammals

Many snakes eat small mammals like mice, rats, and rabbits. Some snakes can eat prey up to three times the size of their own head!

Birds

Some snakes are excellent climbers and can sneak into bird nests to find eggs or chicks.

Certain snakes prey on other reptiles and amphibians, including frogs and lizards. Some snakes, like the eastern indigo snake, prey on other snakes, including venomous ones like rattlesnakes.

Fish

Sea snakes and some freshwater snakes eat fish.

Insects

Snakelets often start their lives eating insects before moving on to larger prey.

Hunting Techniques

Active Hunters

Some snakes, like **cobras** (*right*), use their sharp senses to track down prey quickly. Their long, thin bodies help them move fast and slip into tight spaces.

Ambush Predators

Other snakes, like **puff adders** (*left*), stay still and use camouflage to blend in until prey comes close. Their thick bodies and strong strike make them perfect for surprising their prey.

Constriction

Constrictors like **pythons and boas** (*right*) squeeze their prey tightly, stopping blood flow. Their strong bodies allow them to take on prey larger than themselves and they only need to eat every few months!

Did you know?

Snakes can sense the heartbeat of their prey through vibrations, helping them pinpoint exactly where it is before they strike!

Venom

Venomous snakes like **vipers** inject venom to immobilize prey. Some strike and release, while others hold on until the venom takes effect.

Snake Communication

Snakes are mysterious creatures with complex behaviors that help them survive in diverse environments. While they may not make sounds like birds or mammals, snakes have developed unique ways to communicate and defend themselves. *So how do they communicate without making a sound?*

Pheromones

Snakes use **pheromones** to communicate without making a sound. They release these chemical signals to mark territory or signal to potential mates, sharing messages through the air.

Vibrations

Snakes can feel even the smallest tremors through the ground. This keen sense helps them detect approaching friends or foes, even without seeing or hearing them!

Body Language

By coiling, flattening, or raising their heads, snakes send clear messages to others around them. Whether it's a warning to back off or a signal during mating season, every pose has a purpose!

Defense Mechanisms

In the wild, where danger lurks around every corner, snakes have evolved a variety of strategies to protect themselves from threats. Here's how they stay safe:

Bluffing

When threatened, some snakes like the cobra can adopt a menacing pose, flattening their necks into a hood and hissing loudly to scare off predators.

Camouflage

Many snakes use their environment to hide in plain sight, blending into leaves, sticks, or sand to escape notice.

Escape

If all else fails, a swift retreat often does the trick. Snakes are quick to slip away into tight spaces where predators can't follow.

This cobra's raised posture isn't just for show—it's a defense mechanism designed to make it look bigger and ward off potential threats. It's a bluff that often prevents a confrontation before it can start!

Brumation

Just like bears and groundhogs, snakes take long winter breaks. But instead of hibernating, cold-blooded snakes enter brumation. It's a lighter sleep that lets them save energy while staying ready to wake up if needed.

Hibernation vs Brumation

While warm-blooded animals like bears hibernate deeply to escape the cold, snakes manage their winter rest differently. They slow down, but a warm day might just wake them up!

Did you know?

Some snakes sneak out of their brumation hideouts to sip water and even bask in the sun if a winter day gets warm enough!

How long do snakes brumate?

Snakes can brumate from 2 to 5 months based on their local climate. The colder it is, the longer they might stay tucked away in their cozy winter homes.

Where Do Snakes Brumate?

Snakes often retreat to underground burrows, rocky crevices, or even hollow logs called **hibernacula**. Here, they might huddle with others to keep warm.

Why Snakes Matter

Snakes play a crucial role in maintaining the balance of our ecosystems. As both predators and prey, they not only help **control pest populations**, reducing the spread of disease, but also contribute to **the health of our environment** in ways that affect many other forms of life, including humans.

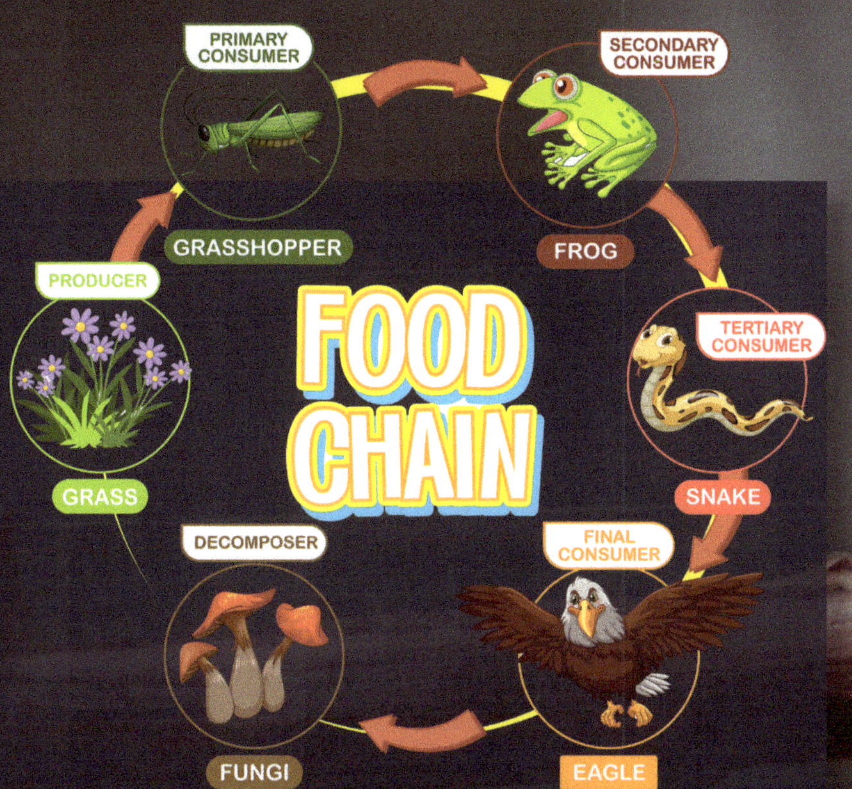

Snakes are important players in maintaining the **balance of nature**. By eating pests like rodents and insects, they help control their numbers, which keeps diseases from spreading and protects crops.

This eating habit also supports a healthy environment for many other animals and plants. Snakes themselves are a source of food for larger predators like eagles. This shows how all parts of an ecosystem work together, with each creature playing a specific role in keeping the environment healthy.

Staying Safe around Snakes

Snakes are amazing creatures, but it's important to stay safe when you're around them. Here's how you can enjoy watching snakes without putting yourself in danger.

Did you know snakes are more active during warmer months? That's when you're most likely to see them out and about!

Snake Safety Checklist

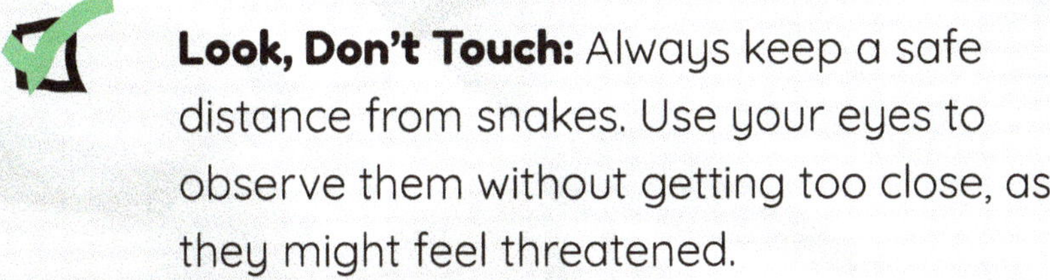

✓ **Look, Don't Touch:** Always keep a safe distance from snakes. Use your eyes to observe them without getting too close, as they might feel threatened.

✓ **Stay on Paths:** Stick to clear paths when walking in nature. Snakes often hide in grass, under rocks, or leaves, so walking on the path reduces surprises.

✓ **Step Carefully:** In areas like rocky hills or dense forests, watch your steps and hands. Use a stick to check bushes or grass ahead of you.

✓ **No Poking:** Never poke into holes or crevices; snakes could be resting there. Treat their homes with respect.

✓ **Seeing a Snake:** If you spot a snake, remain calm and back away slowly. Never try to capture or hurt them—they're usually more afraid of you! **Tell an adult straight away.**

You've already learned so much about snakes, but there's still more to discover! Prepare to dive into a treasure trove of fascinating fun facts about snakes.

Wagler's pit viper

Some snakes like the **green tree python** and the **Kapuas mud snake** can change their skin color depending on the temperature to better blend with their environment, just like a chameleon!

• • •

A **reticulated python** (*right*) holds the record for the longest snake ever discovered. It measured over 30 ft (10m) in length, which is over double the average for the species!

• • •

A snake's heart can move up to a third of its body length to adjust as it swallows large prey. This amazing ability helps them to digest their food.

The **death adder** has the fastest strike of any snake, attacking prey in less than 0.15 seconds.

• • •

Snakes are venomous, not poisonous. This means they use their fangs to inject toxins into their prey to catch them. Poisonous animals, on the other hand, are harmful to touch or eat because they have toxins in their bodies.

• • •

Long ago, some snakes had legs! Fossils of a snake, which was named Najash, show us that snakes evolved from lizards that used to walk on legs.

The common death adder is > native to Australia.

© Petr Hamern

A jungle carpet python.

Pit vipers, **boas**, and **pythons** have heat-sensing organs that detect warm-blooded prey even in total darkness.

• • •

Did you know some sea snakes are expert navigators? They can find their way back to their favorite breeding spots even if it means traveling long distances across the open ocean!

• • •

Snakes have flexible skeletons with hundreds of vertebrae and thousands of muscles for precise movement.

• • •

The oldest recorded snake, a green **anaconda** named "Annie," celebrated her 40th birthday in 2023.

The **Indian egg-eater snake** only eats bird eggs, which it swallows whole using a unique spine in its throat to crack them.

Rattlesnakes can rattle their tails at speeds up to 50 times per second when threatened.

Some large snake species can eat prey up to 75% of their own body weight in a single meal.

Snakes are incredibly adaptable and can live in extreme environments, including the Himalayas where some species such as the **Himalayan pit viper** live at altitudes over 16,000 ft (4876 m)!

The eyelash viper is known for
its distinct "eyelashes," which are
actually modified scales above
their eyes. They live in rainforests
in Central and South America.

The Texas rat snake
is non-venomous and
plays an important role
in controlling pests in its
native Texas.

Did you know that the **annulated sea snake** can breathe through the top of its head? Native to coastal waters around Australia and Asia, this snake uses a special network of blood vessels under the skin of its snout and forehead to draw in oxygen, much like a fish uses gills!

• • •

Snakes have a protective scale over their eyes instead of eyelids, called a spectacle or brille, which helps keep their eyes safe and moist.

• • •

The oldest known snake fossils are over 100 million years old, from the Cretaceous period.

King cobra

Some snake species can lay up to 100 eggs in a single **clutch**! A clutch refers to the number of eggs an animal lays at one time.

. . .

King cobras mostly eat other snakes, even venomous ones. Scientists believe they do this to lower their competition—smart!

. . .

Snakes have more than 10 different slithering techniques to navigate through their environments.

The **anaconda** is the heaviest snake in the world, with some specimens weighing over 550 lbs (249kg)!

• • •

A single snake venom can contain over 200 different proteins and toxins.

A young northwestern garter snake.

Snakes can digest hard substances like bone and feathers due to their strong stomach acids.

Snakes do not chew; they swallow their food whole!

While many snakes have two lungs, some species like the python use only one lung to breathe.

Garter snakes can form large communal dens for hibernation, which may contain thousands of snakes!

Snakes are ectothermic, meaning they rely on external heat sources to regulate their body temperature, unlike humans who are endothermic and can regulate their own temperature. However, some snakes, like those living in the desert, have amazing adaptations—they can change how much blood flows to their skin, helping them stay cool even on the hottest desert days!

• • •

Snakes shed their entire skin, including the scales covering their eyes, in a process called ecdysis.

• • •

Male snakes can be highly territorial during mating season, engaging in wrestling matches to win over females!

Hognose snakes, when threatened, will flip onto their backs and play dead, even letting their tongue hang out to convince predators they're dead.

© Peter Paplanus

The smallest snake species in the world is the **Barbados threadsnake** (Leptotyphlops carlae). It was discovered in 2008 in Barbados and is remarkably tiny, measuring about 4 in (10 cm) in length when fully grown, which is about the size of a large paperclip.

Snakes have a prominent place in many cultures' mythology and symbolism, representing both good and evil. For example, in ancient Greek mythology, the snake is linked to Asclepius, the god of medicine, symbolizing healing and renewal because of its ability to shed its skin. However, in Christianity, the snake is often associated with temptation and sin, as seen in the story of Adam and Eve in the Garden of Eden.

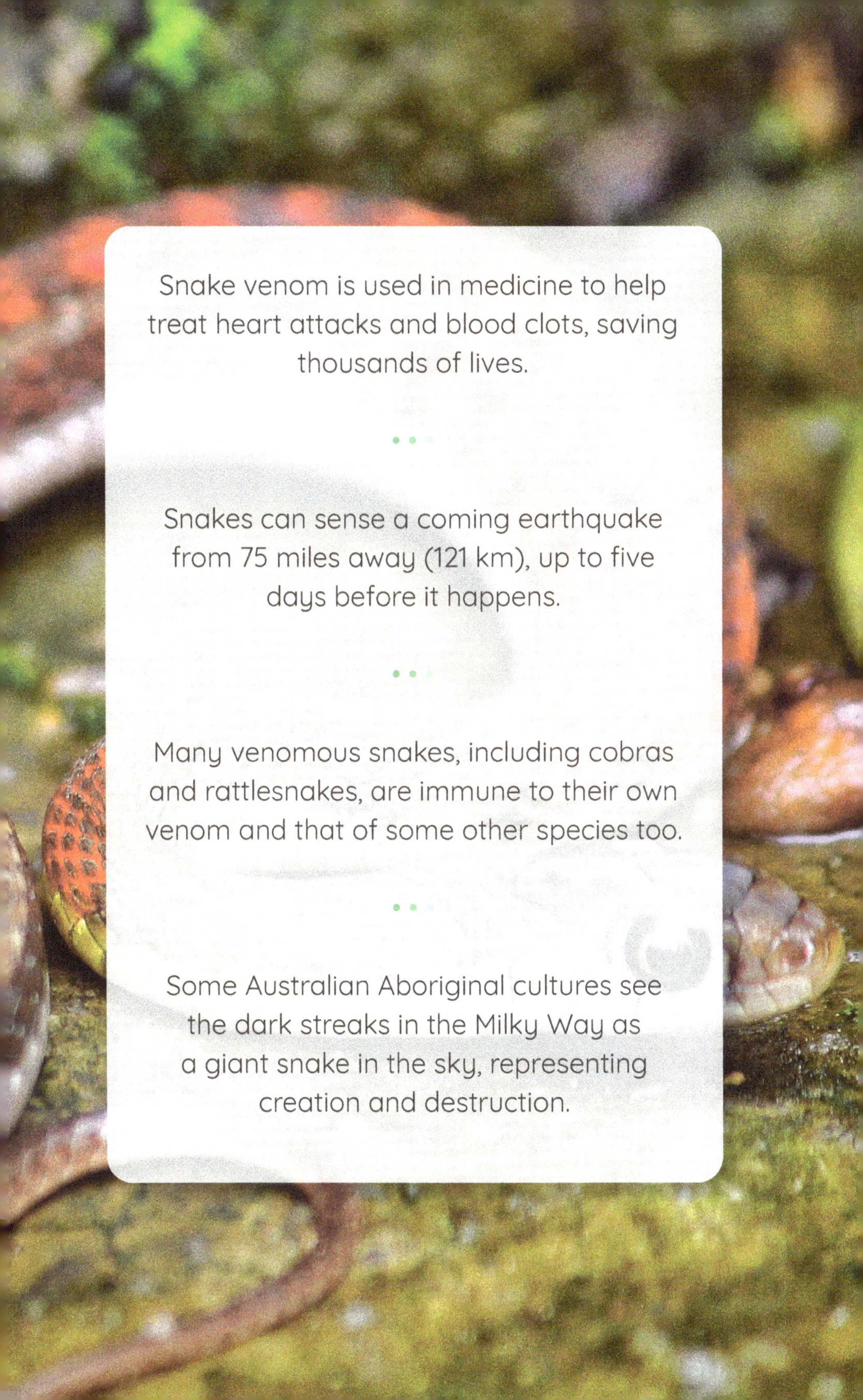

Snake venom is used in medicine to help treat heart attacks and blood clots, saving thousands of lives.

Snakes can sense a coming earthquake from 75 miles away (121 km), up to five days before it happens.

Many venomous snakes, including cobras and rattlesnakes, are immune to their own venom and that of some other species too.

Some Australian Aboriginal cultures see the dark streaks in the Milky Way as a giant snake in the sky, representing creation and destruction.

The **green vine snake** is known for its bright green body and pointed snout, which help it blend in perfectly in its rainforest habitat .

When threatened, some snakes like the
European adder move in a zigzag pattern
to confuse and escape their predators.

• • •

Snakes can close their **glottis** (the opening
for the windpipe) and breathe through a
small tube in their mouths while they eat.

• • •

Snakes are believed to be color-blind,
relying more on movement and heat than
on color vision.

• • •

Being **cold-blooded,** snakes often
sunbathe on rocks to raise their body
temperature and energize for the day.

• • •

A group of snakes is called a **nest** or a **den**.

Snake Quiz

Were you paying attention?! Test your new snake knowledge in our quiz!

1   **What is brumation?**

2   **Are all snakes venomous?**

3   **What do snakes use their forked tongues for?**

4   **Which part of a snake helps it sense vibrations from the ground?**

Answers

1. Brumation is a light sleep that cold-blooded animals like snakes use during cold months to save energy.
2. No, not all snakes are venomous.
3. Snakes use their forked tongues to smell by tasting the air.
4. The belly scales help a snake sense vibrations from the ground.
5. A baby snake is called a snakelet.
6. A nest or a den
7. Sea snakes have salt glands under their tongues to help manage salt intake.
8. Yes, snakes can dislocate their jaws to eat large prey.
9. Ectothermic means using external heat sources to regulate body temperature.
10. The Gaboon Viper has the longest fangs.
11. Desert snakes have specialized kidneys that help conserve water.
12. The purpose of a rattlesnake's rattle is to warn

predators and prevent confrontations.

13. Yes, some snakes can glide from tree to tree.
14. Nocturnal snakes usually have slit pupils.
15. Snakes control pest populations by eating insects and rodents.
16. If you see a snake while hiking, you should stay calm and back away slowly.
17. Snakes smell with their tongues.
18. No, not all snakes lay eggs; some give birth to live young.
19. Some snakes can move their heart within their body when swallowing large prey.
20. Snakes are important because they help control pest populations and are also prey for other wildlife.
21. Cold-blooded.
22. Anaconda.
23. King cobra.

Can you find all the words below in the word search puzzle on the right?

SLITHER	**FANGS**	**RATTLE**
VENOMOUS	**VIPER**	**BRUMATION**
ANACONDA	**SNAKELET**	**SCALES**

Snakes

WORD SEARCH

```
D F X F C H J Y F A S D
Y P J R A T T L E N M F
T S P G X N J H G A N S
R S L B N E G Q A C V C
W N U I Y T R S C O X A
D A Y I T C X Z X N D L
F K T Q D H H G Z D F E
V E E V I P E R T A T S
Z L S C X J T R C Z Q D
V E N O M O U S X X S V
X T B V C Z S D F G H J
C V B R U M A T I O N N
```

Solution

<table>
<tr><td></td><td></td><td>F</td><td></td><td></td><td></td><td>A</td><td></td><td></td></tr>
<tr><td></td><td></td><td>R</td><td>A</td><td>T</td><td>T</td><td>L</td><td>E</td><td>N</td><td></td><td></td></tr>
<tr><td></td><td>S</td><td></td><td></td><td>N</td><td></td><td></td><td>A</td><td></td><td>S</td></tr>
<tr><td></td><td>S</td><td>L</td><td></td><td></td><td>G</td><td></td><td>C</td><td></td><td>C</td></tr>
<tr><td></td><td>N</td><td></td><td>I</td><td></td><td></td><td>S</td><td>O</td><td></td><td>A</td></tr>
<tr><td></td><td>A</td><td></td><td>T</td><td></td><td></td><td></td><td>N</td><td></td><td>L</td></tr>
<tr><td></td><td>K</td><td></td><td></td><td>H</td><td></td><td></td><td>D</td><td></td><td>E</td></tr>
<tr><td></td><td>E</td><td>V</td><td>I</td><td>P</td><td>E</td><td>R</td><td>A</td><td></td><td>S</td></tr>
<tr><td></td><td>L</td><td></td><td></td><td></td><td>R</td><td></td><td></td><td></td></tr>
<tr><td>V</td><td>E</td><td>N</td><td>O</td><td>M</td><td>O</td><td>U</td><td>S</td><td></td></tr>
<tr><td></td><td>T</td><td></td><td></td><td></td><td></td><td></td><td></td><td></td></tr>
<tr><td></td><td></td><td>B</td><td>R</td><td>U</td><td>M</td><td>A</td><td>T</td><td>I</td><td>O</td><td>N</td></tr>
</table>

Sources

Awesome 8: Super snakes. (2021). Retrieved from https://kids.nationalgeographic.com/nature/article/super-snakes

Ballard, H. (2024). How Do Snakes Mate & Reproduce? Are They Asexual or Sexual? Retrieved from https://pangovet.com/pet-health-wellness/snakes/how-do-snakes-mate-reproduce/

Bowie, D. (2024). The Reticulated Python Slithers in as the World's Longest Snake. Retrieved from https://animals.howstuffworks.com/endangered-species/reticulated-python.htm.

Celebrate National Serpent Day With 16 Snake Facts. (2024). Retrieved from https://www.peta.org/features/world-snake-day-snake-facts/

Dan. (2019). Deep breath: this sea snake gathers oxygen through its forehead. Retrieved from https://www.adelaide.edu.au/research/news/list/2019/09/04/deep-breath-this-sea-snake-gathers-oxygen-through-its-forehead

Do Snakes Have Ears? And Other Sensational Serpent Questions. (n.d.). Retrieved from https://nationalzoo.si.edu/animals/news/do-snakes-have-ears-and-other-sensational-serpent-questions.

Garberoglio, F. F., Apesteguía, S., Simões, T. R., Palci, A., Gómez, R. O., Nydam, R. L., … Caldwell, M. W. (2019). Science Advances, 5(11). doi:10.1126/sciadv.aax5833

Graham, D. (n.d.). Discover the weirdest snakes in the world, from flying serpents to spider-tailed vipers. Retrieved from https://www.discoverwildlife.com/animal-facts/reptiles/weirdest-snakes-in-the-world-from-flying-serpents-to-spider-tailed-vipers-theres-even-a-hairy-species

Green tree python. (2024). Retrieved from https://www.dublinzoo.ie/animal/green-tree-python/

Guinness World Records. (n.d.). Oldest living snake in captivity. Retrieved from https://www.guinnessworldrecords.com/world-records/626676-oldest-living-snake-in-captivity.

Hausheer, J. E. (2023). A Field Guide to Commonly Misidentified Snakes. Retrieved from https://blog.nature.org/2019/10/16/a-field-guide-commonly-misidentified-snakes/

Mahony, A. S. (n.d.). Common Death Adder. Retrieved from https://australian.museum/learn/animals/reptiles/common-death-adder/

Person. (2022). 7 cool facts about snakes. Retrieved from https://www.worldanimalprotection.org.au/news/7-cool-facts-about-snakes/

Pskhun. (n.d.). [Herpetology • 2005] Enhydris gyii: Kapuas Mud Snake Retrieved from https://novataxa.blogspot.com/2012/11/2005-enhydris-gyii.html
Snake. (2024). Retrieved from https://www.britannica.com/animal/snake

Snake. (2024). Retrieved from https://en.wikipedia.org/wiki/Snake

Snakes Locate Prey Through Vibration Waves. (2008). Retrieved from https://www.sciencedaily.com/releases/2008/02/080221105350.htm

South Carolina Aquarium. (2023). Reptile Brumation. Retrieved from https://scaquarium.org/brumation/.

Venomous versus poisonous. Same thing, right? Wrong! (n.d.). Retrieved from https://www.nps.gov/cabr/blogs/venomous-versus-poisonous-same-thing-right-wrong.htm.

World Animal Protection. (2022). 7 cool facts about snakes. Retrieved from https://www.worldanimalprotection.org.au/news/7-cool-facts-about-snakes/

Find us on **YouTube** for weekly animal videos just for kids!

Join us on YouTube

You are Sssnake-tacular!

As we reach the end of our epic adventure through the slithery world of snakes, we hope you've enjoyed discovering these majestic creatures as much as we've loved bringing their stories to you.

Your thoughts are incredibly valuable to us, so we would be over the moon if you could leave a review where you picked up this book. Simply scan the QR code below, it only takes a few seconds! Thank you!

Scan me

ALSO BY JENNY KELLETT

... and more!

Available at

www.bellanovabooks.com

and all major online bookstores.